Father Daniel's Compendium of the Undead

Father Daniel's
Compendium
of the
Undead
1st Edition

A **Cry** in the
MOON'S LIGHT

CONTENTS

Father Daniel

of the Abbey at Feldberg

Greetings,

If you are reading this, you have an uncomfortable suspicion: the things of our nightmares are real. You may not fully believe the hunch just yet, but by the time you are done with these writings, you will know the world is full of evil things. These hideous creatures of the night are not just in fairy tales meant to scare children; they exist and have been influencing our world in terrible ways since the beginning of time. We should all be terrified.

Over the centuries, they have hunted, tortured, and killed humans in the most horrific ways. Through knowledge, we understand the nature of the darkness we all face. Ordinary weapons cannot defeat many of these things.

The history you have learned is slightly different than the truth of the past. Places, people, and events are not always what they seem. The darkness has learned to manipulate this world, pitting brother against brother and sister against sister. It has also learned how to rewrite history.

History is written by people with agendas. Kings and rulers, whether influenced by the dark or their own selfish interests, wish to control their people. They rewrite history to fool the masses and keep them from knowing the truth. Those of us who have resisted and believe in truth have committed ourselves to the fight. We have dedicated our lives to the telling of these stories so the enlightened may have their eyes fully opened.

This collection of works is part of the rich tradition of my order. We catalog many things. In this book, you will find a list of confirmed allies to our cause, men and women who have sacrificed much for all of us.

The line between heroism and villainy is often murky, even among night creatures. Some mentioned in this work could be classified as villains—pure evil, with no redeemable qualities. As for the others, I leave judgment up to you.

Our monks have assembled a bestiary of the night creatures and, where possible, included their strengths and weaknesses so you may prepare yourself should you encounter one or two or three. There is also a list of relics we have discovered, some of which we can use to defeat evil and others that evil can use against us. We have included some of the legends and mysteries known to us so you may know them too.

Much of what we know takes place in the major forests of Europe. There is the Black Forest in what is now called Germany. There is the Dark Forest in the South of France, which stretches between the Pyrenees Mountains and the Rhone River. And there is the Great Eastern Forest that stretches from the Rhone River to the eastern lands of Wallachia, where we believe much of this began.

In the late 1700s, many places found themselves in the midst of revolution. In the Americas, there was the War of Independence. France was on the brink of its own revolution. Peasants demanded a better way of life and freedom from ruthless nobles, their outrage nearing a tipping point.

While we know the darkness has infiltrated many kingdoms and governments, it is unknown to us if the dark influenced King Louis XVI's extravagant spending and depletion of the royal coffers. Unfortunately, man is capable of atrocities without supernatural influence. Unlike those who rewrite history, I will provide only accurate information in these writings, and when I am unsure, I will say so specifically.

One truthful tale involved a beautiful young woman who found herself in the middle of a fight between creatures of the night, although she did not know it at the time. In the late *1700*s, she was forced to travel through the Dark Forest as she hurried to the side of her dying grandmother, who lived in a city that no longer exists. On her way, she encountered brutal murders in a hidden village. That village was later destroyed by a corrupt lord who had let the dark into his heart and lost everything in return. His castle was destroyed, his lands revoked, and he was eventually erased from history.

But at the time of this story, the castle stood strong, its secrets buried deep. During her journey, this young woman discovered the truth about the castle and uncovered the mystery of the wolf, which we will tell you later. It was a centuries-old curse that created the first werewolf and sparked the creation of a vast number of hideous night creatures.

This unsuspecting woman found herself in the middle of a conflict between good and evil. At first glance, you might assume that the love she shared with a man was the key to saving all of humanity. But the truth is always more complicated. It wasn't the love of two seemingly insignificant people that ensured the world's survival. It was true love.

These are things not told in the history books of your time. Those tales have been marginalized and labeled as fiction to hide the truth. They're seen as a way to scare children and entertain adults. And they distract all of us from the truth in our politics, lives, and the world.

I hope this guide helps you confront the darkness and the demons you face.

May the Lord bless and keep you.

Father Daniel

ALLIES, VILLAINS, AND THOSE IN BETWEEN

 his is an incomplete list of the many allies in the fight against evil. These are the men and women who have been given the gift of sight and, like you, now see evil, no matter how it tries to disguise itself among us. While many herein have passed, the hope is that they bestowed the truth upon their heirs. May you find them in your time of need.

Also within this section are individuals who may be considered villains as well as those without a clear designation. I leave it up to you to decide whether they are friend or foe, or something else entirely.

✺ Mi Lady ✺
Alessandra d'Harcourt

Generally referred to as mi Lady, Alessandra grew up as a peasant girl in the village of Parlimae, which sat in the shadow of Lord Parlimae's castle. Her family worked the Parlimae lands for many years. She was extremely close to her grandmother.

During her childhood, she was friends with William Parlimae, the lord's only son, and a farm boy named Seth, who she fell in love with. The three were inseparable until her attack.

She was mauled by a black wolf at a young age, and Seth was believed to have died while trying to save her. After a great fire destroyed the village of Parlimae, her family moved to the city of Trevordeaux. Despite the distance, she remained close with her grandmother.

Alessandra later married the Duke of Harcourt, who was also the governor of Normandy.

She was considered to be the most beautiful woman in all of France, yet there are no known paintings of her. We only have a vague description. Various artists have provided sketches of her, which you will find in this text. She had big, brown eyes and auburn hair, and her bright smile made her irresistible to men. Her outward appearance was shy and demure, which hid courage and inner strength.

Alessandra is skilled with a blade, smart, and charismatic. She is as kind as she is courageous. She generally wears a cape and is fond of a perfume made from the red door flower that guards the cemetery behind an abandoned church deep in the forest.

ᏆᎦ Seth ᎧᏌ
Werewolf

Seth grew up a farm boy in the village of Parlimae. He was a strong and handsome young man with blond hair and blue eyes. He was friends with William Parlimae, the only son of Lord Parlimae, when they were both young. The villagers believed Seth was killed while rescuing mi Lady from a black wolf when they were teenagers. But that is far from the truth.

Two men of the nomadic people known as Travellers were hunting in the forest and rescued Seth. Once he recovered from the attack, he learned that the black wolf had killed his family in a fit of rage. With nowhere to go, Seth was raised by the Travellers. But the attack had turned him into a werewolf. The Travellers attempted to hide his affliction by tattooing over the scars he'd gotten from the attack. The magic used to heal him caused the tattoos and his eyes to glow an intense blue in the moon's light.

During an attack on the Traveller camp, Seth attacked his foes, and an unease spread through the group. Unable to stay with the Travellers as they moved on, Seth remained in the Dark Forest. He frequented the hidden village of Mercel and became a highwayman to survive. Nobody knew he was still alive until mi Lady's journey through the Dark Forest.

❧ Captain Francis Altier ❧
Carriage Driver

Leaving home at an early age to earn a living to support his family, the young carriage driver accepted the job to take mi Lady across the country to be with her grandmother. Although he was not handy with a musket or a skilled fighter, he became her protector through the Dark Forest. His courage and loyalty proved invaluable. The perilous trip formed a lasting bond between him and mi Lady, and they became lifelong friends.

After he returned home, the trauma of the journey and the loss of his job proved too much, and he became a drunk. Drifting aimlessly from town to town, he vowed to never return to the Dark Forest. Eventually he took a job on a merchant ship to avoid the evils of land. Working on the docks in Paris, he saved an abandoned girl with mental and physical disabilities from a group of thugs. To protect her and earn a living, he worked to obtain his own vessel. He later became known as Captain Altier of the cargo ship the *Arcan*.

ᔄ Arca ᔅ
Demon Steed of the Witch King

Arca was the lead horse of the carriage team that transported mi Lady through the Dark Forest. He was a coal-black stallion with a white patch above his left eye, a slight imperfection that prevented him from becoming a show horse. Arca's calm nature and intelligence made him a natural leader of the team.

After his death, his spirit wandered through the abyss, making its way to its final destination. The Witch King came across him during this journey and resurrected him. Transformed into a demon steed, he now serves the Witch King, carrying the wicked ruler whenever summoned.

⚜ Pauline "Polly" LaFluer ⚜

Pauline was a young woman in her late teens with a common mental and physical condition that, while unknown at the time, centuries later will become known as Down syndrome. She had long, blond hair, and her eyes had a distinctive slant. Her neck and hands were shortened, but her muscles were well developed, and she was exceedingly strong. Her mental capacity was akin to that of a nine- or ten-year-old child, so she required additional care and support. Her parents died when she was very young. With nobody to take care of her, she was placed in an orphanage.

Mistreated by most, Pauline took to the streets of Paris but found herself in peril early. She made her way to the docks for food. One day, she was forced to fight a group of thugs looking to take advantage of her disability. Captain Altier was working a ship nearby and came to her aid. With nowhere to go and no family to turn to, she accepted the captain's offer to care for her. He unofficially adopted her and referred to her as his daughter.

Captain Altier purchased his own ship when she proved to have a unique aptitude for sailing. He and Pauline developed the ability to communicate with a form of sign language that was invaluable aboard a ship. Her unrelenting loyalty and uncanny ability to keep the ship out of danger caused her to quickly rise to the position of first mate. Captain Altier nicknamed her Polly, partly because she repeated things. Although she had physical and mental disadvantages, Polly was strong willed and clever with a naturally kind disposition. Because of her disability, she was often overlooked. Those who underestimated her usually came to regret it later.

✌ William Parlimae ✌
The Black Wolf

The only son of Lord Parlimae, William hailed from the castle and lands of the same name, located in southern France. He was as handsome as he was spoiled, with strong, chiseled features, a strong jaw, and thick, black hair. He was a sought-after bachelor and enjoyed flaunting his good looks and strength. Although he was friends with both Alessandra and Seth, his sociopathic personality led to an obsession with her and a resentment for Seth.

A hunting trip for wild boar gave him the dark power he needed to act on those feelings. As his party chased their prey deeper into the forest, they were attacked by a supernatural wolf pack. William was exposed to the werewolf curse. He attempted to turn mi Lady into a werewolf, but Seth stopped him. Before he could kill Seth, two Travellers rescued his onetime friend. In a fit of rage, William brutally killed Seth's family as revenge for the interference.

William formed his own wolf pack, terrorizing the village of Parlimae and the surrounding lands. He enjoyed chasing his prey through the forest, feeding on their fear. He was a sadistic killer who derived sexual pleasure from killing. His father's attempts to control him—locking him in the dungeon during full moons—did not always work, and when he escaped, he murdered violently.

❧ Lord Parlimae ☙

He was from the noble bloodline of Parlimae and owned a vast amount of land north and west of the Dark Forest. His wife died during the birth of their son, William, who he protected with reckless abandon. Generally considered a good lord to his people, he provided safety and security to the village at the base of his castle. He knew mi Lady and Seth from their friendship with William as children.

Parlimae was kind and generous but had a blind spot when it came to his son. He was always well dressed and carried himself with pride and confidence. His gray hair and beard were considered handsome, and he was courted by various women in the kingdom, although he never remarried.

✺ Captain Jonathan Barkslow ✺

Captain Barkslow was a former British officer who served with the Hessian Colonel Voelker in the American War of Independence. After leaving the army, he accepted the position of captain of the guard at Castle Parlimae. His experience battling a werewolf in the American War of Independence garnered him a reputation as a fierce fighter. Lord Parlimae hired him to prevent William's murderous rampages during full moons.

Unable to contain William, he turned to Colonel Voelker and the Hessians for help. Without alerting Lord Parlimae, he hired them to kill William—along with any other werewolves in the valley.

Barkslow was a thin man and not very impressive in stature, which fooled most foes. A military man by nature, his countenance exuded confidence. He was regarded as a cunning and capable fighter.

⏝ The Hessians ⏝

The Hessians were an army of fighting men from the Hesse-Cassel region we now know as Germany. Most of the tales we've come across involve Hessians who battled a werewolf while fighting in the American War of Independence. Many were killed in the colonies, but the few who survived returned to Europe, vowing to destroy all night creatures. Although Hessians were normally employed by the enemies of France, these soldiers were mercenaries who fought for whoever paid the most. Though the job had them working on behalf of a French territory, they accepted a contract from Captain Barkslow, agreeing to kill all werewolves in Lord Parlimae's lands.

❧ Colonel Gustav Voelker ❧

Colonel Voelker fought in the American War of Independence alongside Jonathan Barkslow. As a young soldier, he watched a werewolf kill his beloved commander. Voelker returned home to find his mother killed by a witch. The witch kidnapped his brother, Hans, and sister, Greta, with evil intent. Along with two other Hessians, he rescued his siblings and killed the witch. He then hid his sister at the abbey at Feldberg's forge.

Voelker was promoted to the rank of colonel in the Jaeger Corp Cavalry. His obsession with killing night creatures stymied his career, as most people denied the existence of these creatures, and he was labeled mentally unstable.

While France was normally an enemy of the Hessians, he readily accepted the contract to kill werewolves in the lands of Parlimae, vowing to kill all night creatures regardless of who they were or how dangerous they had become.

৩⊙ Pieter and Ishmael ⊙৩
Travellers

The group known as Travellers were a nomadic tribe of people who moved about the forest by caravan. Each wagon was ornately decorated to emphasize the designated job or specialty of the owner. As with other communities, the Travellers elected a king for life, and his word was law. Discriminated against and mistreated by many governments, they preferred to stay away from populated cities and towns. The Travellers were elusive, preferring the deepest parts of the forest and its most secluded areas.

Respected members of the community, Pieter and his son, Ishmael, were hunting red deer when they came across Seth's limp body. They shot the black wolf as he tried to drag Seth into the woods, but they did not kill him. That saved Seth from death. Pieter and Ishmael took Seth back to their community, where the *drabarni* healed him. Pieter then adopted Seth as a son.

৳ Rosalita Amberov ৩

Drabarni of the Travellers

For many years, Rosalita Amberov served as the *drabarni* for the group of Travellers Seth later joined. Hers was an important position within the Traveller community. She was a seer, healer, palm reader, and master of the mystical arts. She was also the keeper of tradition, maintaining the *Book of Soan*. She was revered and respected among her people. Rosalita healed Seth with herbs and magic, then ordered his scars covered with tattoos to hide signs of the werewolf attack. She was the curator of many relics and weapons needed to defeat creatures of the night, such as the dagger of dark silver, the dream catcher, and the crown of thorns.

✒ Anton, Zem, and Tori ✑
Romani of the Great Eastern Forest

The Romani are a community of nomadic people from the Great
Eastern Forest region of Europe, which we now know as Romania. They
were driven from their lands after accidentally crossing into Wallachia
while hunting for food. Night creatures killed most of their people
and chased them to the city of Trevordeaux. While in Trevordeaux, a
Scotsman named Makgill helped them find shelter and food. Anton,
Zem, and Tori entertained pub crowds by playing music for money.
During the battle with the undead, they led a group of peasants out
of the east side of the city and to safety. The remainder of the Romani
escaped with Makgill from the west side.

⨳ Makgill ⨳
The Scotsman

Known as the Scotsman, Makgill is shrouded in mystery. His origins are a bit unclear, though he no doubt came from Scotland. He openly acknowledged being of the Donald clan but denied immigrating with Lord Donald despite their both settling in the city of Trevordeaux. He operated an independent printing press and had vast knowledge of mysterious events in the land. After his building was destroyed by the national guard, he continued to investigate the strange occurrences and published papers detailing the oddities and the murders. He befriended the Romani refugees of the Great Eastern Forest, helping them find shelter and food. He became a strong ally of mi Lady's during the great conflict.

ꙮ The Witch King ꙮ

The Witch King is the most powerful of all witches. Neither his true name nor his exact age is known. Folklore suggests he is centuries old, an undead creature raised by Dark Lord Thocomerius to control the world's witch population because the Dark Lord fears witches.

It has been reported that the Witch King is unable to remember his former life as a human. But one operative believes he was married, as the portrait of a beautiful woman with auburn hair hangs in his castle.

HISTORICAL PLACES
(MANY NO LONGER EXIST)

 he following is a listed description of many places where night creatures have terrorized humanity. Just like other sections, this list is ongoing and thereby incomplete. Some locations no longer exist because of war or other factors. Their importance in the fight cannot be overstated and must be remembered for posterity.

⟶ The Dark Forest ⟶

This vast and dense forest stretches across southern France. A long road runs straight through the middle, connecting the western part of the region to the Rhone River. There are a few smaller roads branching from this main thoroughfare, such as the one that leads to Castle Parlimae. These roads are notorious for concealing road agents and highwaymen, who ambush unsuspecting victims.

The Massif Central Mountain Range borders the forest's northern side, while the Pyrenees Mountains border the south. The forest is very dense, with thick, tall pines throughout. The eastern side of the forest is dense with oak, elm, and poplar trees, which begin to thin as the forest nears Port Calibre. The canopy prevents a lot of sunlight, which allows plants, such as ferns and mosses, to cover the forest floor.

⟶⟶⟶

⟡ Mercel ⟡

Mercel was a small town in the South of France, located in the middle of the Dark Forest. The leafy canopy helped hide its existence, earning it the nickname the Hidden Village. The forest road that connects the west to the Rhone River ran straight through the middle of the town. Mercel was a waypoint for weary travelers who dared enter.

Nobody knows who started the town. Someone built a rough cabin as a place to get out of the elements. Someone else built a store to sell supplies. After that, an inn with a pub was constructed to accommodate travelers.

Mercel was not officially recognized as a town by King Louis IV. There was no lawman or military for protection, which made it a hangout for road agents and highwaymen. Crime, however, was kept to a minimum in the town itself, a concession made to avoid attracting the king's attention. Justice was swift and often lethal.

King Louis IV took an interest in Mercel when it burned to the ground, and he did not permit the town to be rebuilt. Eventually, it was forgotten.

⟡⟡⟡

⋯ Castle Parlimae ⋯

Also known as the Falls Castle, this was a majestic structure built into the side of a mountain within the Massif Central Mountain Range. A giant waterfall cascaded to the west of the structure and emptied into a large ravine. This expanse ran in front of the castle, making the only known access by way of the drawbridge.

The Parlimaes owned the surrounding lands for generations. The village of Parlimae rested in the shadow of the great castle. The peasants there worked the fields, which bordered the Dark Forest. Villagers and artisans sold their goods within the castle walls and throughout the village. The markets of Parlimae were well known throughout the South of France.

A secret dungeon had been built into the castle long ago. At the time of William Parlimae, it was used only to contain William during a full moon. His crimes, and the atrocity Lord Parlimae committed when covering up those crimes, eventually led to the destruction of the great castle. All memory of it has been erased from the history books.

⋯⋯⋯

···→ The Abandoned Church ···→

Deep in the Dark Forest, not far from the hidden village of Mercel, there once existed another village. It was abandoned so long ago that its name has been forgotten. An abandoned church is the only structure left and the only indication that a town once existed there.

When they were younger, Seth and mi Lady used to visit the ruins during their long rides in the forest. When Seth was forced to leave the Travellers because of his affliction, he often hid in the abandoned church.

After Seth rescued mi Lady from the black wolf on a nearby beach, he brought her to the abandoned church as a safe place to heal. The road leading to the church was well hidden by forest vegetation, making it an ideal place to hide.

···→

⁘ The Cemetery ⁘

An old cemetery lies behind the abandoned church, deep in the Dark Forest. An unknown people built the stone wall that surrounds the small burial grounds. A few gravestones mark the final resting place of people long forgotten.

A unique black-and-red flower grows around the outside of the cemetery. It has red thorns that are poisonous to both humans and night creatures. The iron gate leading into the cemetery is covered with the flowers, blanketing it in red. Seth refers to the gate as the red door.

Careful not to come into contract with the deadly flower, mi Lady and Seth often hid in the cemetery when they wanted to be alone.

⁘⁘⁘

⤙ The Beach ⤚

Near the end of the Dark Forest, before it hits Port Calibre, lies a small stretch of beach. Here, France meets the Mediterranean Sea. It is the location where the black wolf and his pack nearly killed mi Lady before she was rescued by Seth.

After healing at the abandoned church, mi Lady fled with Seth toward the city of Trevordeaux. They intended to pass by the beach but were waylaid by the Hessians. A final confrontation with Colonel Voelker ensued.

⟡⟡⟡

⟶ Port Calibre ⟶

A small seaport town, Port Calibre was situated on the Mediterranean Sea in the South of France. It sat at the edge of the Dark Forest and served as the gateway to the city of Trevordeaux. The Rhone River emptied into the sea here and allowed for smaller boats to travel upstream to Trevordeaux. Captain Altier's ship, the *Arcan*, often delivered goods to Port Calibre.

While the town still exists, the name has been changed to erase its involvement in the great conflict.

◆—◆—◆

⟶ The City of Trevordeaux ⟶

Trevordeaux was the last major city in southeastern France. The Rhone River ran through its middle, separating the city into two major sections. Although the river was fast moving, merchants delivered goods and services to the docks there.

The west side was inhabited by the wealthy aristocracy, while the peasants lived on the east side. A large stone bridge connected the sections, allowing workers from the east side to walk to the various businesses on the west side.

Most cultural amenities were on the west side. A large park served as the city's central hub. It had an outdoor amphitheater as well as an indoor playhouse on the northwest corner.

Local government offices were in the city building on the southwest corner. The city library was located on the square and widely considered to have one of the best collections of reading materials outside of Paris.

Saint Pierre's Cathedral was on the southeast corner, boasting high steeples that could be seen from as far away as the Dark Forest. Although the bells were forbidden from ringing after the revolution, it still held regular mass up until its destruction.

King Louis XVI considered this city a major hub of his kingdom's commerce, so much so that he assigned a garrison of national guard to provide security for the city. The national guard barracks and stables were on the southern edge of the city. This provided easy access to the docks as well as the road to Port Calibre.

Fields owned by nobles were to the north and west. Rolling hills stretched all the way to the Dark Forest, while flatter fields to the north reached the Massif Central Mountains. The Great Eastern Forest bordered the east side.

Despite the city's onetime importance to the kingdom of France, it no longer exists.

◆—◆—◆

⤙ The Forge ⤚
Abbey at Feldberg

Long ago, a large silver mine was constructed within a mountain in the Black Forest. Those aware of night creatures mined the precious metal to create weapons against the evil beasts. The darkness began to forcibly take silver shipments to prevent the creation of these weapons.

Monks then built a giant forge to make the weapons the moment the silver was mined. An abbey was carved into the side of the mountain, high above. It's where the monks reside and continue their devotions.

To protect the forge and abbey, a citadel was constructed at the base of the mountain, overlooking a canyon. This guards the abbey and the forge against intruders. Like so many places during the war with the undead, it was later destroyed to prevent its true purpose from being known. Blessed with the knowledge of the secret of silver, monks from the Right Hand of God Order create some of the most lethal weapons against night creatures. They also record their findings in books such as this one, which was compiled by Father Daniel.

⬦⬦⬦⬦⬦

⟶ Blackmoor Castle ⟶

A great deal of mystery surrounds Blackmoor Castle, which is located near the center of the lands we now know as Romania. Built atop a mountain and surrounded on all sides by miles of swamp, the castle is accessible only by a narrow road that snakes through the bog and to the foot of the mountain. From there, the road continues up steep inclines to the castle.

The expansive bog is littered with the corpses of animals and humans alike. A perpetual fog covers the flatland, and no matter the time of day, it is always gloomy.

Beasts known as the Apeshi, or Hairy Ones, inhabit the Great Eastern Forest that lies just beyond the bog. Their whoops and tree knocks make for an eerie journey. Giant bats are often seen flying over the swamp in search of food. And hellhounds patrol the narrow road as well as the forest. They kill anything that approaches, dragging their victims into the thick fog until the screams can no longer be heard.

Those who lived to tell of their time at Blackmoor describe it as a large structure with no defensive walls. At the apex of the mountain, the narrow pass meets large, steel doors that provide entry. Inside, there is a wide staircase with lush, red carpeting. A chandelier with one hundred candles burns in the center of the foyer.

The grand ballroom on the first floor is used for celebrations. It's where most guests are permitted. The main dining hall is across the foyer and holds several long tables. A massive firepit burns in the middle of the room.

In the foyer, a door behind the staircase leads to an iron elevator that takes passengers to the lower levels. Some say this provides entry to catacombs where undead creatures roam. We also believe the Witch King's black forge, where he creates unimaginable weapons, is somewhere in these depths. A river runs beneath the castle and connects the bog to the Black Sea.

Nobody has been able to describe the upper levels of the castle. Rumors have persisted for centuries, some claiming that the Witch King's laboratory exists up there. Music echoes through the swamp, and some people believe it emanates from the upper levels.

The lands surrounding Blackmoor Castle are considered private, and anyone wandering too close is deemed a trespasser. Very few have ever found the castle. There are no known maps. Each time a map is created, something destroys it. We nearly lost our entire library to a suspicious fire after one of our monks sketched a map based off a witness's description.

◆·◆·◆·◆·➤

MAPS

his section contains a collection of the maps of the world as they existed before men of power decided they should be changed. We begin with a map of the world as we now know it so you may see the difference and what was lost.

Official Map of Eastern Europe and Southern France

EUROPE, 1800

Map of Eastern Europe and Southern France Before History Was Rewritten

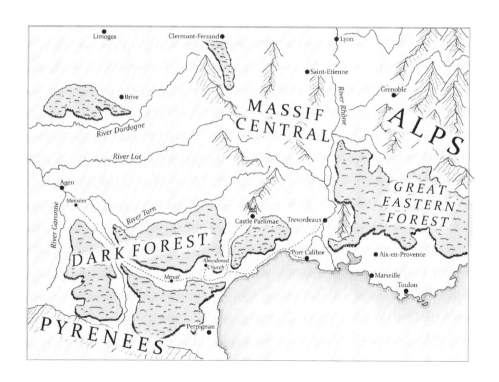

Trevordeaux

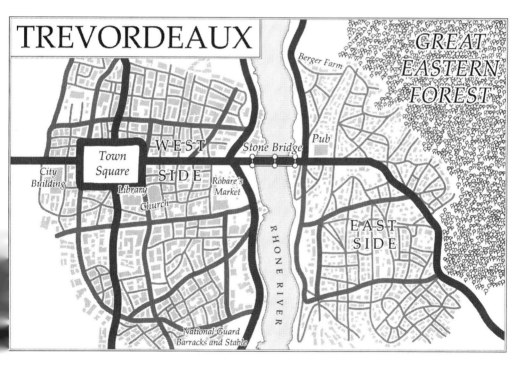

BESTIARY

 ur monks have diligently prepared this section to provide you with the most current information we have on the monsters. Many are creatures we have fought directly, while others we have not encountered. For those entries, we have included information from various eyewitness reports and sources to help you.

We have provided you with descriptions of these beasts so you may be able to recognize them. And while we hope you never encounter them, we thought it important that you understand their strengths and weaknesses in case you find yourself facing any of them. Most are unable to defend against fire, but no weapon is quite as effective as the metal ore silver. It kills nearly all night creatures when it pierces the heart.

Each monster has a purpose or class. Many are warriors. Some are used for strength. And others simply spread chaos. Regardless of their caste, all terrorize and frighten. Make no mistake about it: all of these monsters are deadly fighters and will kill you without hesitation.

Be advised that a lot of these creatures have been discussed throughout history but marked as folklore. Disinformation about their authenticity and vulnerabilities abounds. Rest assured that what you read in this bestiary is the most up-to-date information we can provide.

You should be aware that many of the creatures are created by evil or magic, sometimes both. For this reason, new creatures we have not encountered yet may exist.

⅋ Werewolves ⅋

These creatures are shape-shifting humans who transform into a half-man, half-wolf or full-wolf form. The affliction is caused by an attack from another werewolf. A victim's intense fear during the attack increases the odds of contracting the disease.

Werewolves first came into existence through a witch's curse. A full moon compels the change, although they are able to transform at will, any time of the day or night. Their healing ability is uncharted, but their blood has been known to cure humans.

They are nearly impossible to kill because of their supernatural strength, which they gain by absorbing their victim's life force at the time of death. When werewolves assume full-wolf form, they lose some strength, but their speed increases because they can move on all fours.

In addition to supernatural strength and speed, they possess heightened senses of sight, smell, and hearing. They can reach a height of seven to nine feet and weigh between eight hundred and a thousand pounds. Werewolves have large, wolflike heads and bodies covered in fur. Large teeth and strong jaws support a superior bite force. Their eyes are generally amber, except for most alpha leaders, whose eyes are red.

A second witch's curse turned silver into a viable weapon against werewolves. While all silver inflicts harm, the purest silver does the most damage. Dark silver is lethal when it strikes any part of the body, but any silver that reaches the heart will kill the beast, leaving only the dead corpse of a man.

⅊ Witches ⅊

These supernatural beings are generally—but not always—human. Witches possess the knowledge and skills to control magic through spells, incantations, and the harnessing of energy. This ability is commonly referred to as the practice of witchcraft, which is punishable by death in most lands.

They're often raised in groups known as covens or recruited at a young age. Witches can be male or female, though males are sometimes called sorcerers or warlocks.

To work their magic, witches use herbs, spells, and natural energies of the world. Sometimes spells require old languages that must be spoken in certain tones in order to work. Sacrifices are common, as blood is at the heart of most rituals.

Practitioners of white magic generally utilize their powers to heal, predict the future, and create better outcomes for those around them. White magic is typically predictable, using energy and items from the natural world in a harmonious way. Though the magic often requires sacrifice, lower animals usually are sufficient.

Practitioners of black magic use dark energy as a weapon. They have the ability to summon demons and direct evil. Black magic is often unpredictable and difficult to control. There is always a price for using black magic. The darkness is clever, allowing a witch to see only what it wishes. Consequences are often undisclosed.

Darkness and evil thrive on strong negative emotions, such as greed, anger, jealousy, envy, and the array of deadly sins. This can lead to vengeance and murder. Sacrifices for successful spells in black magic involve predatory animals, including humans. Generally, the eviler the sacrifice, the more effective the spell.

The most-advanced practitioners of witchcraft possess the knowledge and ability to raise the dead. Some are capable of creating all types of evil creatures, each with unique abilities to serve the witch's needs.

Witches are natural enemies of vampyrs and werewolves, but they will use magic to control or create these creatures if it serves their purpose.

❧ Witch King ❧

The Witch King possesses unparalleled expertise in the use of black magic. He is also an accomplished necromancer, using his ability to create night creatures that he deploys around the world. They serve as spies, create chaos, and spread fear among the humans.

He created and commands the Army of the Undead, which is virtually indestructible. His pet phoenix resurrects any creatures felled in battle, thereby preventing the loss of any of his soldiers.

The Witch King forged his own armor and primary weapon, leading some to believe he was a former blacksmith. He carries a bladed pike constructed of dark silver. A cross structure high on the spear allows the phoenix to perch in battle.

He harbors an extreme hatred for werewolves, one of the few night creatures he did not create. His left eye is missing, and three large claw marks rake down his face—both reminders of a previous fight with a werewolf. He shaves the left side of his head as a reminder of the battle and normally wears a dark silver mask on the left side of his face.

The vast majority of his creations, be they creatures, weapons, or relics, are made at his home, Blackmoor Castle. Few travelers have returned from a visit to his castle. Those who have are generally unable to remember details of their visit or how to find the castle. We believe he casts a spell on those he permits to leave, which interferes with their memories.

Over the centuries, there have been a few grand balls and celebrations at the castle. World leaders attend but usually return with foggy remembrances of the event. The Witch King's reasons for hosting these events are not clear, but leaders go with hopes of preventing him from using the Army of the Undead against them.

⚜ Phoenix ⚜

Also known as the Resurrection Bird, this creature was created by Dark Lord Thocomerius as a gift for the Witch King. It aides him in raising the Army of the Undead. The bird is consumed by intense blue and black flames that can melt the strongest metal, making weapons ineffective and armor little protection. Silver might be effective, but it turns to liquid long before reaching the phoenix's heart.

The bird is capable of reviving the recently deceased whenever they are felled. Almost nothing can resist the flame as the bird pulls them from the depths of hell to serve again. This allows the Witch King to continually replenish his army, even when humans use a creature's weakness to defeat it.

But the phoenix doesn't just resurrect slain night creatures; it's also capable of raising humans and animals killed on the battlefield. Each time a creature is brought back to life, the bird consumes a piece of it, causing the onetime human or animal to come back as the undead. The Witch King doesn't hesitate to recruit them into his Army of the Undead.

When silver weapons are used to kill night creatures, however, the Resurrection Bird is unable to bring them back.

The Witch King has grown fond of the bird and keeps it close by. He is the only entity capable of tolerating the intense heat of the flames. And his pike is the only weapon known to be able to kill the bird.

Aside from the Witch King's weapon, we do not know of any of the bird's weaknesses. We suspected water would be a weakness, but it turns to vapor upon contact with the creature. Many theorize that the bird would die if submerged for a length of time long enough for water to put out its flame.

⚔ Meridious ⚔
The Green Ghost

Meridious is the name of the Witch King's personal servant, a ghost who sees to the needs of the Witch King at Blackmoor Castle. He appears as a green specter. During grand balls and other events, he directs the function of the castle and its many ghoulish inhabitants.

Meridious is tied to Blackmoor Castle and therefore unable to leave its walls. He's usually dressed in the elaborate clothing of a lead house butler: a long coat and fancy shirt. Though he is totally devoted to the Witch King and incapable of betraying him, he seems to convey a sympathy for mankind. Meridious is one of the few creatures not created by the Witch King but bound to him for unexplained reasons.

Those who have encountered Meridious report he is pleasant yet formal. They provide no information about how to dispatch him but say he does not appear to be a threat to humanity. Some speculate he may be an ally, if such a thing exists in the darkness.

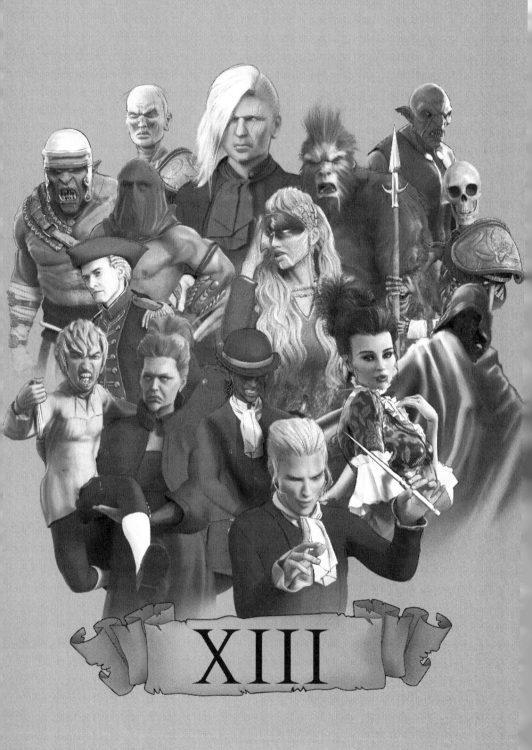

⚜ Council of Thirteen ⚜

We know of at least thirteen different types of night creatures that the Witch King has created. Each hideous beast has unique strengths and weaknesses. The Witch King has the ability to control them either telepathically or through the use of some type of magical instrument. But he prefers to give his order to the members of the Council of Thirteen, each of which controls its respective race of the undead and directs its battalions to carry out the Witch King's commands. Only Dark Lord Thocomerius can override an order by the Witch King. Throughout the centuries, whenever his army has been used, the Council of the Thirteen has been at his side.

From what we have ascertained, these are the members of the council:

1. Whisps Speaker
2. Alp Leader
3. Goblin Imp Child Nanny
4. Wretch Commander
5. Chieftain of the Apeshi (Hairy Ones)
6. Ogura Boss
7. Ossa Bellator Captain (skeletons)
8. Larua (ghosts) Whisperer
9. Water Goblin Prince
10. Brugorus Kennel Master
11. VOAs Conductor
12. Vampyr Supremo
13. Human Sympathizer General

⚚ Whisps ⚚

Ghoulish, ghostlike creatures that can phase in and out of reality—and disappear from sight—are known as whisps. Some who have encountered the beings say they've heard a quick whooshing or whispering sound during this transition. Others have described hearing a low murmur or mumble when a whisp is near.

They wear ragged, hooded cloaks of a greenish-black color. Their hoods are always up, shadowing their faces. Most humans are unable to look at a whisp's face without suffering psychological trauma. Long, black, wiry arms with sharp, black claws extend from under their capes. While their legs are thin and black, they appear to hover over the ground.

Using their ability to remain completely hidden from view, they whisper suggestions in the ears of their victims, who often carry out the evil ideas. The consequences can be deadly. For this reason, whisps make excellent spies and infiltrators.

Whisps have few known weaknesses. While they hover at various heights above land, they do not have the ability to pass over water or liquid. If a silver weapon penetrates the area where the heart belongs, it will kill a whisp—even if the creature phases out of reality or becomes invisible.

Whisps generally work alone or in small numbers. They possess great strength and prefer tearing their enemies apart with their sharp claws. They enjoy being coated in the blood and guts of their victims. Despite their viscous nature, they are mainly used to create chaos and mistrust in an enemy.

⚡ Alp ⚡

This demonic creature can appear as any number of living things, including a human. The main source of an alp's power is a magical object known as a tarnkappe, or hat of concealment. Folklore suggests it is a cap, but our research shows the translation is too literal. We have encountered female alp whose magical concealment object is a hair bow. As long as the creature wears the magic item high enough on its person, it can influence how it is perceived. Those who are enlightened can sometimes see an alp's amber eyes through the veil of illusion.

Legends state the creatures only come out at night, but we know this is not true. The Witch King has been placing alp in various governments and monarchies around the world. These creatures are one of the main instigators of the evil that men do.

The alp influence humans in any number of ways—causing nightmares, for instance, or capitalizing on human weaknesses, such as gambling or sex. Alp often use seduction as a method to control both men and women. If they are unable to gain direct access to leaders, they will often entrap senior advisors to influence the desired leader.

There are no documented cases indicating how an alp is created. Several theories have evolved after circumstantial evidence pointed to birthing by a human host. According to sources, the gestation period is so short that a woman will believe the delivery was a dream, never realizing she gave birth to a demonic being. Many believe the Witch King creates a potion that is given to an alp who then impregnates a corruptible woman.

The Witch King is not the only creator of alp. Witches skilled enough to wield black magic have been known to create a potion that allows them to create alp.

When it comes to defending against alp, silver harms, and dark silver kills. They prefer to remain undetected, which suggests they fear being killed. If you are able to catch one, you may be able to trick it into leading you back to its master. It is our advice that if you find an alp in human form, mark the creature and wait for it to become inactive. Then place a lemon in its mouth when idle to control it. Some report that this can incapacitate them.

⚘ Goblin Imp Child ⚘

A hideous and grotesque supernatural being, the goblin imp child (GIC) is small in stature. With the frame of a child and a penchant for children's clothes, it is impossible to distinguish them from a human child when glimpsed from behind.

They usually have blond or white hair that touches their shoulders, dark green skin, red eyes, and sharp, ultra-white teeth. They frequently smile, feeding off the first moment of terror in a human or animal. Their long, yellow fingernails usually grip a shiny blade, which they use to cut their victims. They carry a gemmed goblet so they can collect the blood of their victims and quench their insatiable thirst.

GICs enjoy removing victims' lips and eyes as well as various patches of skin, leaving the bodies where they'll easily be found. The mutilated bodies give rise to terror, and GICs feed off it.

The creatures are exceedingly strong and can leap great distances. They often climb or leap into trees to avoid being seen. They can climb walls or ceilings with ease.

While most hideous creatures avoid the daylight, GICs are known to attack at all times of the day or night. Their weaknesses are water and silver.

⚡ Wretch ⚡

Wretches are deceased humans reanimated with magic. The Witch King is believed to have created the first wretch. Since that time, other witches, warlocks, and some human sympathizers have learned the technique. These creatures are void of a soul or mind and would wander about aimlessly without the direction of the wretch commander.

They're prone to eating flesh and bone, but because they're too slow to catch prey, wretches trap victims and devour them, leaving no trace. Their skin is often rotting and discolored, with missing chunks of hair and flesh. They are extremely slow moving and easy to outrun.

A wretch's only strengths are its tight grip and jaws made for tearing the flesh off its victims. They experience no discomfort or pain, so they're able to relentlessly pursue their prey, but the slightest barrier can foil their pursuit. They are able to walk underwater, but a faint current is enough to carry them away.

Wretches' weakness is daylight. Much like a vampyr, they cannot function in direct sunlight. As dawn approaches, they dig effortlessly into the earth and lie dormant until the sun goes down. Although they should not have the strength to dig, the earth moves to give them shelter.

Aside from sunlight, the only thing that can destroy a wretch is silver. They will alter their course to avoid touching any silver because the metal, when driven through the heart or brain, will kill them. Death is not often permanent for these monsters; they're easiest of all night creatures for the Resurrection Bird to bring back. But not even the phoenix can reanimate a wretch if it has been killed with silver.

⅄ Apeshi or Hairy Ones ⅄

The Witch King deploys these apelike creatures to forest regions all over the world. Apeshi are primarily used to scare people and keep them from exploring areas of the forest the Witch King wants to keep hidden.

These are large creatures, standing over eight feet tall and weighing over a thousand pounds. Their bodies are covered in fur, and while their coats can vary in color, they're normally dark. Most have brown eyes, but some apeshi's eyes are red.

They're believed to be highly intelligent creatures. They usually carry clubs, which they use to knock against trees as a form of long-distance communication. Whoops and yips have also been heard and may be additional ways apeshi communicate.

The creatures hide or eat their kills. They are omnivores and will eat anything, including small pets and children. People often disappear in woods they are known to inhabit.

Despite being enormous, they are very agile and quick, with an uncanny ability to hide. Some believe they have mind-control abilities, which would explain how they disappear from view. They have the ability to mimic the sounds of forest animals, such as owls or coyotes. They have no known weaknesses, but we believe conventional weapons will kill them.

⚡ Imprimir ꝑA ⚡
Ogura

The exceedingly large, manlike monster called the imprimir PA is also known as an ogura. They're reportedly twice the size of the Hairy Ones, with short legs and an oversized trunk. The head is large, the teeth big and square, and the eyes red. Their skin is normally a greenish yellow, but there have been sightings of rare red oguras, which are more temperamental.

They usually carry double-bladed axes and enjoy killing humans. Ogura like to eat humans but have a real taste for small children and infants. They rarely come out during the day, but daylight is not a weakness. They are slow and cumbersome in their movements, but they make up for it by being extremely strong. The Witch King uses them as muscle in his army. Their size and strength make them ideal for moving large objects or smashing structures.

Ogura skin is thick and nearly impossible to penetrate. As far as we know, only silver can cut through their flesh and harm them. Unlike the Hairy Ones, ogura have little to no intelligence. They require constant guidance to carry out the most trivial of tasks.

⚹ Ossa Bellator ⚹

Also known as skeletons, ossa bellators are similar to wretches in that they possess no measurable intelligence and need direction to complete tasks. But unlike wretches, they are better at following orders and, while slow, can maneuver around and climb over obstacles.

Skeletons are the exposed frames of humans, but they are not the cleaned, white bones seen in Halloween costumes or medical schools. Held together by very thin pieces of tissue and tendon—along with a bit of magic—an ossa bellator's form is usually covered with bits of flesh and stains of blood. Occasionally the bones will hold an eyeball or hair that has not completely rotted away.

Although they do not eat or devour any type of food, ossa bellators are relentless in pursuit of prey and kill anything that crosses their path with a ferocity unmatched by the other creatures. Skeletons use weapons such as swords and muskets they find along the way. They are known to carry shields to protect against attack.

Ossa bellators do not do well in sunlight. Just like their cousins, the wretches, they burrow in the earth right before dawn and rise when the sun goes down. They are not as weak as wretches but do not possess superior strength. They are impervious to fire and are known to walk through flames without an issue.

A musket ball or sword strike to certain locations on the skeleton can topple them. Weapons of silver, thrust into the area of the ribcage that used to hold the heart, can kill them permanently.

While they are not intelligent, they are capable of thought and rudimentary reasoning. But they have no compassion or independent judgement. Their only purpose is to kill and to obey their masters.

⚜ Larua ⚜

Larua are disembodied souls with evil intent. While they can pass through objects, they can also control matter in our realm. This gives them the ability to move things without revealing themselves, which causes terror among those who encounter them. Imagine seeing a sword swinging in the air by itself.

Some appear in their prior human form, while others take on the grotesque appearance of various hideous beings. These creatures are as varied as the gender and races of all living things. Humans with proper knowledge can summon them from the astral plane. With the correct incantations, a human can force larua to show themselves, countering the creature's ability to remain invisible. They are able to directly speak and communicate with humans, especially in the devil's tongue.

Laruas enjoy killing humans by tricking victims into some form of self-harm. Many believe this is a source of amusement to them. They are hard to control, stubborn, and unruly because they do not wish to remain in this realm. They carry out the orders of the Witch King without hesitation, making them good in battle. It is believed the Witch King possesses some type of amulet that compels them.

Larua are impervious to all known weapons, except dark silver and salt. Ordinary silver does not harm them. Contact with salt injures them, and they cannot cross a salt barrier. Too much exposure to salt sends them back to the depths of darkness.

Some are unable to leave certain areas, while others are tied to a person. None of them can cross large bodies of water, and while sunlight is not believed to harm them, they are rarely active during the daytime.

⚹ Water Goblin ⚹

Humanoid half-man, half-fish creatures are called water goblins. They reside in large bodies of water and have gills instead of lungs. Water goblins can walk on land but cannot survive long out of water. They have been known to come on land to attack.

Extended webbing on their hands and feet allows them to move swiftly through water. Large, round scales provide warmth, which makes them ideal for cold waters and the murky deep.

The scale also serves as armor, making it difficult for bladed weapons or arrows to pierce their bodies. Musket balls have been successful, but silver to the heart is the best way to kill them. Fire is a known weakness for times when they're on land.

Similar to sharks, water goblins can smell the smallest drop of blood in water from miles away. Anyone with a cut or injury who is swimming within range becomes prey.

They enjoy feeding on young, virile men, normally attacking from below and chewing off the genitals with razor-sharp teeth. After the victim is injured, they drag the body to the depths of the water and stash it under a rock to tenderize the meat.

Water goblins are rarely seen during daylight hours. Sunlight burns their skin even under the water.

⚡ Brugorus ⚡
Demon Dog

The brugorus is a large, bone-crushing, bearlike, doglike creature. Most who encounter the creature say it appears to have clawed its way from hell—which, of course, it has. It's described as having dark and matted fur, a heavy tail, large teeth, and a strong jaw supported by an over-sized head.

Later, paleontologists, such as Frenchman Édouard Lartet, labeled it *Amphicyon*, but it's commonly called the bear dog or demon dog. Its red eyes and murderous nature are always absent from descriptions written by men of science, who simply explain away the supernatural origin of this creature.

We know this monster to be the creation of the Witch King. Demon dogs are reportedly his favorite creation. Many ancient battles describe seeing the skeletal form of these creatures, further demonstrating the Witch King's fondness for them.

The Witch King is known to combine creatures to produce hideous monsters with the traits he needs. In this case, he uses the dead corpses of wolves, bears, and monitor lizards.

Demon dogs avoid water, although it's not believed to harm them. Sunlight does not appear to harm them, but they avoid the daylight. People who have survived an encounter did so during the day. Witnesses claim their escapes were aided by sunlight.

They are fast and see so well in the dark that some believe they can see through solid objects to locate prey. The Witch King uses them to track victims because they have a superior sense of smell. They are often seen in the company of the apeshi. When they're not in battle, they patrol the Witch King's lands and roam Blackmoor Castle, killing invaders.

Most night creatures do not attack other night creatures, but demon dogs have been known to strike at other monsters, although nobody has been able to explain why. They only obey the Kennel Master and the Witch King. No other being, living or undead, has any ability to control them.

⚡ Voice of Angels ⚡

Its name suggests divine origins, but this is a very sinister monster, designed to lure unsuspecting humans to their death. The creature's melodic tones sound like the voices of angels (VOA). Many cultures have reported variations of these dangerous creatures throughout recorded history. The Greeks told tales of creatures whose song lured nearby sailors and caused shipwrecks.

Byzantines described them as females with large wings similar to those of a sparrow and a song that would lure men into the forest. Others describe them as singing men to sleep and then tearing them apart. Even Leonardo da Vinci described these beings in his notes.

We know very little about their true appearance. Those who have lived through an encounter describe them as beautiful, which helps to further distract their victims. According to survivor reports, VOAs use melodic sounds to alleviate fear and tension. This causes an almost trancelike state for victims, who then wander in the direction of the sounds. Some report VOAs kill directly, while others maintain they merely bring victims to the other monsters.

⅋ Vampyr ⅋

These are grotesque, soulless, undead creatures that somewhat resemble humans. Their skin is so pale it is nearly white, making it susceptible to burns from the sun's rays. (Sunlight does not kill them, despite what folklore suggests.) Their eyes are pink and sensitive to light of all kinds, so it is difficult for them to contend with the daylight.

Vampyrs possess superior strength but need blood to remain strong. They survive by drinking the blood of humans and animals, emerging at night from caves and dark places to feed on any living creature. Extremely fast and agile, they are difficult to kill. Despite what various legends claim, they are not shapeshifters with the ability to change form.

There are two types of vampyrs: originals and their grotesque descendants. An advanced practitioner of witchcraft aiding the first ruler of Wallachia, Thocomerius sought aid from the God of Shadow. In a bargain to defeat his enemies, Thocomerius became the first vampyr.

Dark Lord Thocomerius remains beautiful and strong beyond compare, as do the originals he created. But vampyrs created after them are hideous, hairless monstrosities with pasty skin and a ravenous appetite for blood.

Thocomerius created a vampyr queen, who has the ability to communicate with all vampyrs in ways we do not yet understand. She created more queens, who in turn create soldiers. Scholars liken the hierarchy to a hive of bees.

We believe the infliction is transmitted through saliva or other fluids. A bite turns the victim into a vampyr. Such easy transmission may indicate a large vampyr population, but we do not know how many hives exist in the world. Also unclear: how many vampyrs are in each hive. Some appear to have as few as three members, while others have hundreds. Our information suggests there are dozens of hives in various countries. Every culture has its own name for them.

Vampyrs are difficult to control, and each hive is fiercely independent. Some of our operatives have noted that the Witch King appears to have a commander, known as the Vampyr Supremo, in his Council of Thirteen. We believe this is the first vampyr queen.

Human Sympathizers

These might be the worst and most deadly creatures of all. These humans have sold their souls to the devil in exchange for power, wealth, and eternal life. They conspire with the Witch King and other night creatures. These men and women typically have vast resources that the Dark Lord requires. Some even become his servants.

Their strengths are wealth and power. Some are world leaders, while others have influence with world leaders or command huge armies. Their weaknesses include human frailties of the flesh and mind.

⸸ Dark Lord Thocomerius ⸸

We believe Thocomerius to be the first vampyr. It is also believed he is the first vaivode, or military commander, of Wallachia. Not much is known about him beyond his harsh rule of Wallachia. He took a bride early and sired several children. After he mistreated the peasantry, his subjects joined with the Golden Horde to remove the cruel king.

With the help of a witch advisor, Thocomerius sought the God of Shadow's aid in crushing the invasion. In order to defeat his enemies, Thocomerius needed an invincible army. He also needed supernatural abilities to control the army. The god granted him immortality with the condition that he consume human blood. He received mind-control abilities to communicate his orders to the creatures, as well as superior strength, blinding speed, and complete regenerative powers. With these abilities, Thocomerius could command the army and rule Wallachia as long as he wanted.

The Dark Lord cemented the deal with a contract etched in stone and his own blood. As promised, a demonic Army of the Undead rose up and crushed the Golden Horde. But it also ruthlessly killed all of Thocomerius's family except for one male child. The peasants were framed for the murders, further cementing his hatred for humanity.

⚘ God of Shadow ⚘

An all-powerful and evil being, the God of Shadow enjoys the torment of man. Some claim to hear a voice from the Kingdom of Darkness, where the God of Shadow reigns. Without true form and unable to cross over to our realm, it uses proxy demons and creates eternal evil creatures to carry out its wicked plans.

There is much disagreement about the God of Shadow among members of our order. Some believe it is one of the archons closely related to the rule of a planetary realm. Others believe it is one in a group of archons that includes Satan himself.

Regardless of what this evil entity is or where it comes from, we agree it impacts our world in destructive ways. It has no apparent purpose apart from creating wicked chaos.

It is strongest at night or in dark places. The God of Shadow's frailty in the light is passed down through its creations and in its contracts.

LEGENDS, MYTHS, AND MYSTERIES

hroughout recorded history man has tried to explain the things he did not understand. Sometimes stories of events take on a larger-than-life aspect. Other stories are pure fabrications that become believed by the masses. The Dark Lord has used these techniques to sow distrust in the peoples of the world in an effort to hide the truth. Our monks have compiled many of these stories and recorded the facts so you may know the truth in these tales.

❧ Legend of the Wolf ❧

Centuries ago, a cruel king from an area beyond what was once called the Great Eastern Forest lived through a revolution. His people joined an invading army to overthrow him, but they failed. During the conflict, the king's family was killed. Driven to madness by the loss, he unleashed an unspeakable evil into the world.

The king permitted his noblemen to commit atrocities against the people. One of the cruelest of them all made a fatal mistake that changed history. He defiled a young woman on her wedding day, a subject he thought meek and helpless.

Distraught by the nobleman's actions and his inability to stop them, the woman's husband killed himself. With her young family destroyed, she took her revenge. What the nobleman hadn't known was that she was a witch. She turned the wicked nobleman into the first werewolf.

Every full moon, the nobleman turned into the beast. He infected others, who then passed on the disease, creating more werewolves over the centuries. But a werewolf's evil goes beyond creating other werewolves.

During full moons, the nobleman transformed and slaughtered peasants. He visited terror throughout the land, much to the delight of the wicked king. The werewolves he created were equally vicious.

One such werewolf terrorized the Dark Forest region and became known as the Beast of Gévaudan. It is believed to be responsible for over five hundred deaths in that area alone. The king dispatched hunters to kill it. Francois Antoine shot a large wolf and put it on display at the king's court in 1765. Little did they know that this was not the beast.

A decade later, the killings resumed. This time, they moved slightly west, occurring in areas of the Dark Forest that lay closer to the lands of Parlimae. The beast's killings were underreported because the landowners didn't want the king to send any more professional hunters to the region.

The curse was not contained in this area of the world. A werewolf was unleashed in the Americas and killed many soldiers during the American War of Independence. It decapitated a Hessian leader, who rose from the grave and later became an evil spirit. This creature, known as the Headless Horseman, terrorizes those lands to this day.

❧ Secret of Silver ❧

It has been widely known for centuries that silver harms most night creatures. Silver will cut flesh, crush bones, and burn skin. Most night creatures will survive and heal from these wounds unless the silver reaches their hearts. When silver pierces the heart—or the space where the heart used to be—a night creature will die. This is the final death, and not even a necromancer or the Resurrection Bird can bring them back.

The use of silver to destroy night creatures started when the witch's curse turned the cruel nobleman of Wallachia into the first werewolf. She did not realize how powerful a supernatural being could be. Evil has a way of enhancing power, slightly altering the deals it makes with humans.

Most night creatures are harmed by man-made weapons but rarely killed by them. That miscalculation cost the witch more of her family, so she created a new curse. In order to fight the supernatural being, she needed supernatural weapons. She convened her coven and placed a curse on the nobleman's silver, the purest form of the metal known to man. Then she forged weapons from the cursed silver and used them to slay the beast.

Though the witch only cursed the nobleman's silver, the black magic attached itself to all the silver in the world. This is the reason any silver weapon can harm night creatures.

The purer the silver, the more damaging it is. Yet both ordinary silver and pure silver have limitations. The witch did not pour enough darkness into the curse, which is why you need to hit the heart in order to kill a beast.

But there is another form of silver that is more lethal than ordinary silver or even pure silver: dark silver. This form of the metal takes the witch's curse much further. We believe the Witch King created dark silver in a forge at Blackmoor Castle. Given the Witch King's mastery of forging weapons, we believe he was a former blacksmith.

His skills support that theory. As a practitioner of the dark arts, his ability far exceeds that of all other witches, enabling him to summon massive amounts of evil, which he then pours into silver during the smelting process. Once a sufficient amount of darkness is infused into the metal, the silver turns black. He then hammers the ingots into blades and hones them to razor sharpness.

A dark silver blade will kill a man just as any other knife, sword, or axe would. But the effects are devastating to night creatures. When a night creature is cut by a dark silver blade, the wound never heals. The essence of the creature pours out like blood until the beast is no more. All night creatures fear dark silver because they have no defense against the evil in these blades.

We do not know how much dark silver exists in the world but believe it is finite. We know of a dagger that was created in the fifteenth century. The Witch King's favorite weapon is a pike with a dark silver blade. There is a cross segment of the pike that serves as a perch for the phoenix during battle. The phoenix is the only creature that does not fear dark silver, as all metal turns to liquid when it comes in contact with the intense heat of the bird's flames. Its fire is so powerful that the Witch King's pike would melt beneath the bird's fire were it not for a spell that protects it against the heat.

❦ Legend of the Vampyr ❦

Over the centuries, there have been many legends of vampyrs. Different cultures tell different versions, some influenced by monarchs who use the tales to create fear and control their people.

One such legend was born out of propaganda designed to unite forces against a vicious ruler. Vlad Tepes, who went by Dracula, was known to brutalize enemies by putting their dead bodies on pikes and displaying them prominently across his lands. He became known as Vlad the Impaler. Four centuries later, a young author named Stoker used this legend to weave a tale of an undead creature that drinks blood and only comes out at night.

Unfortunately, these fictional characterizations do not assist us in defeating the very real entity that is the vampyr. These hideous creatures are neither charming nor beautiful, as romanticized throughout the centuries.

The first vampyr in our record is the Dark Lord Thocomerius. He was the first ruler of Wallachia, which is now known as Romania. During an uprising in his land, all but one of his children were killed, a loss that drove him mad. A mage advisor skilled in the dark arts prompted Thocomerius to summon the God of Shadow. He struck a bargain with the ancient and evil entity, exchanging his soul and undying devotion for the defeat of his enemies and vengeance for his family's deaths. In the process, Thocomerius became a servant of this evil.

The God of Shadow killed Thocomerius then resurrected him as a vampyr, the first of his kind. Unlike vampyrs of legend, he is not affected by sunlight. He is not a shape-shifter, nor does he sleep in a coffin.

Lord Thocomerius no longer eats food as we do. He only drinks blood—any type will do, but he prefers human blood. His incisors were turned into fangs, and when they penetrate the skin, a gland in his mouth secrets an enzyme that thins the blood for drinking. This also infects the victim with vampyrism. Victims who do not die from blood loss become creatures similar to Thocomerius.

The Dark Lord's appearance did not change much. His skin turned pale, and his teeth gained fangs, but he was otherwise the same. Similarly, his first victims changed only slightly in appearance. The women became more beautiful, now undead and never to age.

The remainder of the vampyrs, however, take on a very ugly appearance. They lose their hair, and all their teeth become fangs. Their eyes turn pink, and they develop a sensitivity to light. While they do not burst into flame, sunlight injures them and can eventually lead to a final death. Vampyrs do not like water. Holy water, or water that has been blessed by a bona fide holy man, burns them and can cause death if it reaches the heart.

Despite old myths about stakes, there is no evidence to support the theory that wood can kill them. Vampyrs have uncharted healing abilities, just as werewolves do. The only way to defeat them is by injuring their hearts or using certain weapons and elements.

Silver injures and kills. Dark silver is the ultimate weapon, as a cut from one of these blades does not heal. Even if it's not struck in the heart, a vampyr cut by a dark silver blade will bleed out and suffer the final death.

The other method of permanently killing a vampyr is to behead the creature. Generally any sharp object will do, but they have tough skin. Silver is the only known substance that slices through their skin with ease.

Vampyrs serve the one who created them or turned them. They operate much like a bee colony. A queen creates workers or slaves, and they obey her. Only Dark Lord Thocomerius can override a queen's command. They possess great strength and speed but, despite what legends say, cannot shape-shift.

❧ Legend of Sleepy Hollow ❧

As with most folklore, there is truth behind this tale. In 1820, an American author named Washington Irving published this story as a fictional work, changing many of the actual details. It is unclear if this was a writer's embellishment or if other forces influenced him to fictionalize the tale, thereby misdirecting people and suppressing the truth.

During the American War of Independence, Gustav Voelker was a jaeger in the deadly Hessian army that fought for the British in an area known as New York. As he and the other infantrymen were marching through the country on their way to a battleground, they encountered a werewolf deep in a dark glen.

The creature killed many of the men and beheaded their commander. The Hessian and British soldiers who survived, including Voelker, returned to their homelands to recount the events. Voelker's courage in battle helped him rise quickly to the rank of colonel, but his career stalled as he became obsessed with killing night creatures.

Since that time, reports of a Headless Horseman roaming the dark glen surface from time to time. Some have even reported the horseman carries a will-o'-the-wisp to terrorize witnesses. It is believed this horseman—the spirit of the Hessian commander, is unable to rest and is compelled to take the life of anyone who travels through that dark area.

❧❧

❦ Hansel and Gretel ❦

Upon returning to Hesse-Cassel from the American War of Independence, Gustav Voelker found his mother slain and his brother, Hans, and sister, Greta, missing. He learned from the Grimm brothers that a witch had taken his siblings. The men helped Voelker and two of his surviving Hessian comrades track the witch to the Black Forest.

The three Hessian jaegers and the brothers Grimm found the witch with Hans and Greta at her house in the Black Forest, not far from the abbey at Feldberg.

The two brothers later published this tale but changed most of the facts. The Grimms renamed the children Hansel and Gretel and described them as being abandoned in the Black Forest. In the tale, they're taken by a cannibal witch, who fattens them up before she tries to eat them. Hansel tricks her, and the siblings escape.

We know the tale to be much darker, with an ending that's not nearly as happy as the brothers Grimm tell it. The true account of this tale can be found in volume two of *A Cry in the Moon's Light*.

❦❦❦

❧ Matty Groves ☙

Matty Groves was a young man who had an affair with a married woman in the city of Trevordeaux. The woman's husband, Lord Donald, learned of the affair, which led to dire consequences. This tale has been the basis of a troubadour song for over a century, though it goes by different names. We believe the God of Shadow used one of his minions to bring this song to life, attracted by its macabre premise and using Matty Groves, Lady Donald, and Lord Donald as unsuspecting participants. Since the tragic events in Trevordeaux, the minstrels have been playing the song more frequently, titling it "Matty Groves."

❧ 8 ☙

Mystery of the Undead

The majority of night creatures are of the undead variety. Long ago, the God of Shadow and other demonic creatures were vanquished to the depths of hell. Although they are unable to take form in our realm, their influence is found everywhere.

Unsatisfied with the unpredictability of man's obedience, they elected to control creatures that lacked morals. These are the undead beings that inhabit the dark places of our reality. The power of a necromancer brought many such creatures to form. They behave as if alive, yet they are not.

The undead include whisps, wretches, vampyrs, and others of their kind. Although they are deceased in every sense of the word, they still perform functions as if they were alive. The Resurrection Bird, or phoenix, is responsible for a vast majority of the reanimation that occurs, but those who possess the knowledge of witchcraft and black magic are capable of creating undead beings.

Humans fear these creatures because they are already dead, believing that nonliving creatures cannot be killed. This is not entirely true, as certain weapons and other forms of magic can remove the undead from this plane of existence. We call this the finite, or certain, death.

While it is extremely difficult to defeat these creatures, silver, dark silver, holy water, blessed relics, and other means can vanquish these abominations.

❧ Magic and Spells ❧

The practice of magic as we understand it can be traced back to the Key of Solomon. Magic is the art of using energies found in the natural and supernatural realms to go beyond science and faith. We think of magic in two forms: white and black.

White magic is generally used for the benefit of others and in pursuit of positive outcomes. Black magic is used for evil purposes and often serves the will of the dark. At times, however, black magic can inadvertently arrive at good outcomes.

While some possess a natural aptitude in the practice of magic, it is generally a learned skill. Both humans and nonhuman supernatural beings are capable of proficiently using magic to attain their goals.

Most magic relies on spells, which can involve specialized ancient languages that harness the energies of the earth and heavens. It is well known that practitioners can wield sound waves for good or evil. Consider a pitch high enough to shatter glass. While this is a rudimentary example, incantations utilizing the proper language, pitch, and tone are effective in summoning the powers of magic.

Natural energies contained in roots, plants, and animals are often incorporated into spells and curses. Spells generally last a finite amount of time, whereas curses can go on for centuries—or until the curse is broken via an anti-spell.

An object can be infused with either white or black magic, depending on the practitioner's purpose for the object. Most of the time, objects are given strength or a new power.

The most damaging of all types of magic is the black magic of necromancy, the ability to reanimate dead animals or humans. When most of a being's soul has departed, the art of resurrecting the being requires specialized skill. Practitioners of this level are considered masters of the art.

❧ ❧

RELICS, WEAPONS, AND OTHER STRANGE THINGS

 s discussed in previous sections of this book, the night creatures all have weaknesses that can be exploited. This section contains descriptions of the various relics and weapons that can be used for that purpose. Some have magical properties that will help you locate or see those things that wish to remain hidden. Others are weapons that can be used to kill the things that seem unstoppable. We have employed artists to draw pictures of these strange things so you may easily identify them for acquisition should you need them in the coming battle.

∽ Silver ∽

For centuries, this precious metal has been coveted and used as a source of wealth. Silver is easy to mold, and metalworkers create ornate works of art in dinning utensils, pots, vases, carvings, and other signs of wealth. It is also used as coins, onto which the most pretentious of monarchs engrave their images.

The purest silver ore is found deep in the earth and is mined under hazardous conditions. This ore holds a deep luster and reflects the light very well. The best silver mines in the world are found in Spain.

A witch's curse enhanced the metal's ability to capture and hold daylight, making it the most effective weapon against evil monsters. Mere contact with silver harms most night creatures, and the purer the silver, the more damage it can inflict.

∽

∼ Dark Silver ∼

By using black magic to infuse the darkest evil into the purest silver, a witch can create dark silver. We believe there are only four or five practitioners in the world who possess enough skill to create dark silver. The evil used in the process renders the metal black, hence the name. Once the spell is concluded and the dark silver ingots are turned, the metal is shaped into weapons.

A cut from a blade made of dark silver never heals. Victims will bleed or ooze life force until they are dead and unable to exist on this plane. None of the night creatures can withstand a cut from a weapon forged by dark silver. Only the phoenix appears to be immune, as the metal melts before it comes in contact with the firebird.

～ Dagger of Dark Silver ～

One of three known dark silver weapons still in existence, the blade was forged long ago, but we do not know when or by whom. The *drabarni* of the Travellers became the protector of the blade until she gave it to Seth.

A gem of enhanced blue sapphire is embedded in the pommel. We call this the Blue Moon Sapphire, and it is the only of its kind in existence. It is believed the gem serves as a prism that directs the moon's light into a narrow beam powerful enough to burn straight through the flesh of night creatures. This is only achieved during a full moon. Additionally, if the conditions are right, looking through the gem can reveal hidden night creatures.

Isaiah 40:29 is inscribed in the handle: He giveth power to the faint; and to them that have no might he increaseth strength. We do not know who inscribed this King James Bible verse into the handle, but it leads us to believe the weapon may have been blessed. This is unconfirmed, as it was forged using evil.

∽ Red Door Flower ∽
Rosa Atra Mortis
Black Rose of Death

A member of the rosa genus, the Rosa Atra Mortis has black petals with red accents. It grows on a long vine with red thorns that secrete poison. Nothing is immune to its deadly touch, including other fauna and certain night creatures—hence its nickname, the Black Rose of Death.

The flower only grows in certain areas of southern France. The most notable is a cemetery behind an abandoned church hidden in the Dark Forest. The Rosa Atra Mortis grows all around the cemetery, preventing anything from passing. The flower grows so densely on the gates to the cemetery that locals call them the red doors.

Seth liked the scent of the red door flowers so much that Alessandra had the petals harvested and the oil extracted to create a perfume she wore. Because of its rarity and deadly consequences, this flower was never included in Joseph von Hammer-Purgstall's *Dictionnaire du Language des Fleurs*, which in 1809 became the first published list associating flowers with symbolic definitions. Nor was it included in *Le Langage des Fleurs*, the first dictionary of floriography, which Louise Cortambert, writing under the pen name Madame Charlotte de La Tour, published in 1819.

∾ Sunlight ∾

Take heed, as there is little to the trope that sunlight kills all night creatures. While some perish in its light, most hideous beasts avoid sunlight because it is easier to hide during the night or in dark places. Some find it hard to maneuver in the sun's heat, while others have trouble seeing in the daylight.

The God of Shadow and his minions avoid the day for these reasons. Some night creatures suffer when exposed to too much sunlight, but it does not necessarily kill them. Many will burrow into the ground and wait until night to attack. Sunlight represents truth and openness, but do not be fooled into thinking it means safety too. That is simply not true.

～ Water ～

Water is one of the few known weapons effective against night creatures. Holy water (that which has been blessed by a priest, cardinal, or pope) is very potent, burning and repelling the beasts. But blessings only take to small batches of water. Large bodies of water, such as lakes, rivers, and oceans, never retain blessings.

We do not fully understand water's impact on night creatures. As most are undead, they do not need oxygen to breathe, but they have trouble maintaining their footing in swift-moving currents. Ocean waves and swift rivers are impossible for many to cross. Still waters and small creeks are not an issue, and one should not be fooled into believing these are barriers.

There are night creatures whose domains are bodies of water. They navigate well in all types of water and hide in the murky depths, awaiting their prey.

⁓ Crown of Thorns ⁓

The original crown of thorns placed on Christ at the crucifixion is a sacred relic in Christianity. It was preserved and eventually brought to France by Baldwin II, the Latin emperor of Constantinople. He offered it to King Louis IX, who built the Sainte-Chapelle to house relics like the crown of thorns. It remained there until the French Revolution, during which it disappeared.

This is believed to be the most effective weapon against night creatures, its power exceeding even that of dark silver. Unfortunately, we do not know where it is right now. But if one could retrieve the true crown, the thorns would kill any of the undead with ease.

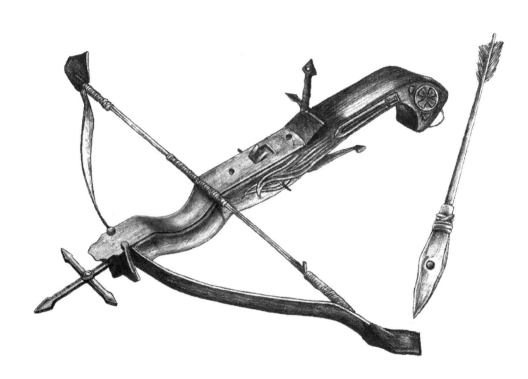

～ The Right Hand of God ～

After it was initially broken apart, wood from the cross used in the crucifixion of our Lord became indestructible. Fragments were deposited in many of the world's great cities, and a few ended up in France. Unfortunately, most of these wood shards have gone missing. The remaining pieces were crafted into sacred relics, which are extremely potent weapons against evil, especially the ones soaked with the blood of Christ.

The monks at the forge created a powerful crossbow made of rosewood and silver, the latter of which prevents night creatures from wielding it. One bolt was created using a shard of wood from the cross where Jesus's right hand was nailed. The hole in the wood is still visible on the bolt. The blood of Christ soaked this piece of wood, making it a deadly weapon against evil. The bolt is indestructible. Even fire cannot harm this sacred piece of wood.

The monks who created this weapon refer to themselves as The Right Hand of God Order.

~ Glasses of Revelation ~

Although we do not know who forged the dagger of dark silver, a few pieces of the Blue Moon Sapphire were acquired by our monks. We were able to fuse the gem with glass and form a pair of spectacles. These glasses can pierce the veil of deception used by night creatures, revealing their true forms. The frame is made from silver to prevent night creatures from handling it. It is the only known pair in existence.

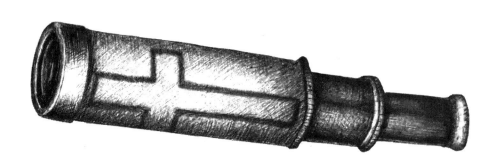

~ Spyglass of Veil ~

The remaining piece from the Blue Moon Sapphire was forged into this spyglass. Using other pieces of glass to enlarge faraway objects, the special gem filters the images and permits the viewer to see the true form of a night creature. The spyglass is heavy in construction and laced with silver to prevent evil from destroying it.

~ Tarnkappe ~

An alp will wear this magical hat to hide its true form. The magic embedded in the cap of concealment allows the wearer to project upon itself any image it wishes. While most alp use this magical object in the form of a hat, female alp are known to use a ribbon or bow in their hair to achieve the same effect. The higher on the wearer the tarnkappe is placed, the better the illusion. Once a tarnkappe is removed, the true form of the wearer is revealed.

∾ Dream Catcher ∾

The common use for dream catchers comes from the First Nations people of the Americas. Fabric, hair, or other items are woven into a net or web. The object is traditionally hung above beds to catch bad dreams and filter good thoughts.

The nomadic peoples of Europe have started to infuse these designs with white magic. Often they act as an instrument with which a user can commune with other realms. Generally it is believed the design of the webbing directs the intended usage.

~ Book of Soan ~
Spells Occult Astrology Necromancy

The *Book of Soan* is a volume filled with occult and ceremonial magic. The authors are unknown. The book has been handed down through several generations of Travellers, its safekeeping always left to the *drabarni*.

The book contains recipes for spells (primarily white magic), magical uses for herbs and bones, and specific instructions for creating an effective dream catcher. Its pages describe certain poisons and weapons useful against the undead, as well as herbs and techniques to heal the living. It also contains a very detailed demonology guide.

The book was lost in the great war with the undead. It is believed the spell to create dark silver was contained within this book, and its loss is the reason so few pieces of dark silver have been created. Francis Barrett later compiled a book he called *The Magus*, or *Celestial Intelligencer*, which included much of what the *Book of Soan* contained. Nobody knows where Barrett obtained the information.

❧ Grimoire ❧
Book of Spells

A grimoire is a textbook of magical spells that contains instructions for creating various charms and magical objects, such as amulets. A darker section of this book teaches how to summon demons and create night creatures. It is believed Thocomerius's witch advisor possessed such a book and used it to summon the God of Shadow when Thocomerius was turned into the first vampyr. Many believe the spell that created the first werewolf was contained within a grimoire, as was the spell that turned silver into a weapon against the undead.

～ Witch King's Dark Silver Pike ～

The primary weapon of the Witch King, this long pike is constructed of the strongest known metal and infused with the purest silver. He forged the weapon at Blackmoor Castle, forming its bladed tip from dark silver. A horizontal section a few feet below the top serves as a perch for the Witch King's phoenix. Etched into the staff and perch is a black magic spell in the language of Sheol. These dark writings protect the shaft from being destroyed and from melting under the intense heat of the firebird.

This weapon is capable of killing all night creatures and, because of the spell cast upon it, the phoenix. With silver running through the staff, no creature but the Witch King himself can wield the pike. And with the dark spell protecting the staff, humans cannot use it either.

THE ART OF A CRY IN THE MOON'S LIGHT

I wish to acknowledge the many talented artists who provided their skills for the world of *A Cry in the Moon's Light*. Here at the abbey, our monks compiled the many legends and stories before you. To give you a fuller experience, we ventured outside our stone walls to various artists and have included their work in the telling of this story.

We have included those who wished to be named, as well as places to find their work. Most provided addresses on something called the World Wide Web. We are not familiar with such a place here at the abbey and erroneously believed it was some type of giant web by a magical spider. This does not appear to be the case. We were told it was part of something called the Internet. We thought perhaps this was some type of netting on Captain Altier and Polly's ship, the *Arcan*, but that does not appear to be the case. Unfortunately, we cannot advise you as to what this is but simply offer the language as presented to us by the various artists. There are some who declined to be named, and of course we respected their wishes.

I wish to thank all those who have contributed to this compendium and works of *A Cry in the Moon's Light*.

Emily's World of Design

Provided the cover design. Emily can be found at a place known as 99Designs.com.

Brian Blacketer

Provided the graphic novel art contained herein. Brian can be found on something known as Instagram at @brianblacketer.

Johnny Haxby

Provided the many character designs herein. More of his art can be viewed at JohnnyHaxby.art.

Morrigan A. Harrington

Provided many of the illustrations contained in the bestiary. She can be found at @madebymomo on something called Fiverr.

Mirjahon Kenjaboyev

Provided many of the scenic and environment pieces. You may find more of his work at MirjahonKenjaboyev.artstation.com.

Patigonart

Provided the artwork for the dagger of dark silver and red door flower, as seen on the cover and in the Relics, Weapons, and Other Strange Things section. This artist can be found on something called Fiverr or artstation.com.

Dewi Hargreaves

Created the maps found in this book. Dewi's other works can be found at DewiHargreaves.com.

Mairys Jasel

Created many of the relics and weapons. You may find more of her talent at @Pabstia on something known as Instagram.

Ammie Govers

Provided artwork that appears in the Legends, Myths, and Mysteries section of this book. Her talents can be found on Instagram at @aliella_fantasy_art.

Patrick Boyer

Provided the cover art for the podcast. More of Patrick's art can be found at UrbanCowboy.net.

Joseph McDade

Provided the soundtrack for this book and podcast. Joe can be found at JosephMcdade.com.

If you would like to listen to a narration of book one of this story, you may find it in the form of something called a podcast, available where most podcasts are found. The enhanced audiobook is in podcast form and includes sound F/X and original music.

The original musical score can be purchased on most streaming services. This album also features a poem written and narrated by Alan McGill.

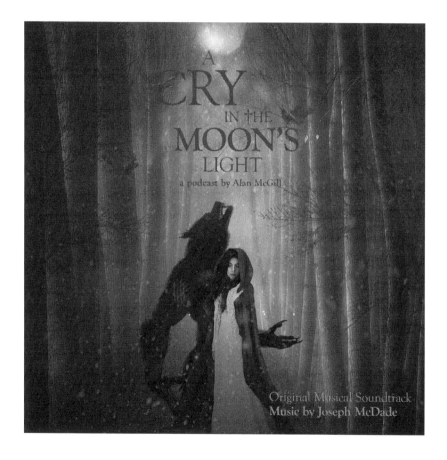

THANK YOU

Thank you for reading this illustrated guide to *A Cry in the Moon's Light*. If you've already purchased the main title or have listened to the podcast, I hope you found the sections of this book enhanced your enjoyment of the story. If you have yet to purchase it, I hope the pages herein have intrigued you enough to get a copy of the book or tune into the podcast.

I hope you enjoyed the numerous illustrations found within these pages. Each artist worked hard and provided their talents to enhance the experience of this tale.

If you enjoyed it, please consider providing a short review on Amazon, Goodreads, or any other location. Reviews and likes make the story more accessible to other readers and are invaluable to the success of these works.

For more information on future stories, adventures, and other things, please follow me at

    @AlanMcGill14

    @AlanMcGill14

alanmcgill.com

acryinthemonslight.com

You can also listen to an audio version of *A Cry in the Moon's Light* as a podcast at cryinthemoonslight.podbean.com or wherever podcasts can be found.

The story is narrated by me, with original music provided by Joseph McDade. If you like the score, you can listen to it on most streaming services.

ABOUT THE AUTHOR

Alan McGill is an American author who lives in northwestern Pennsylvania with a clowder of cats. Alan was close to his grandparents, who grew up during the Great Depression. They were married young and remained together until his grandmother's passing. His grandfather served in the Navy during WWII and was a gifted storyteller who wove humorous tales about tough events. Alan grew up listening to these stories of right and wrong and watching fictional heroes—such as the Lone Ranger, Adam West's Batman, and Captain America—stand up to bullies and protect those who could not protect themselves. This inspired him to always do what was right in his own life and shaped his love of storytelling. He is a multi-genre author whose debut novel, *A Cry in the Moon's Light*, combines horror, romance, and mystery. As with all his books, *A Cry in the Moon's Light* centers on characters who strive to do the right thing regardless of the adversity they face. The book focuses on the theme of love—a pure and deep love that defeats all evil.

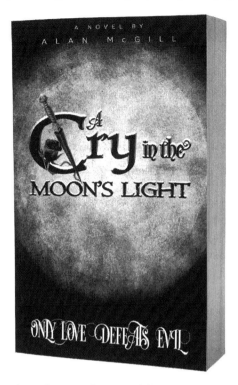

Made in the USA
Middletown, DE
31 December 2021

57282718R00109